# Frosted Glass

## Denys Cazet

☆ Bradbury Press ☆ New York ☆

The text of this book is set in 14 pt. Congress. The illustrations are drawn in
pencil with watercolor wash, reproduced in full color.
Printed and bound in Japan.
Book design by Sylvia Frezzolini.          2  3  4  5  6  7  8  9  10

Library of Congress Cataloging-in-Publication Data: Cazet, Denys. Frosted glass. Summary: Gregory the
dog's vivid imagination gets him in trouble at school, leading him to draw cities and spaceships when he
should be doing something else, but his artistic ability does not go unrecognized.   [1. Imagination —
Fiction.   2. Drawing — Fiction.   3. Schools — Fiction.   4. Dogs — Fiction]   I. Title. PZ7.C2985Fr
1987     [E]     86-26822     ISBN 0-02-717960-5

for Kyran

Gregory touched the window.
The glass was cold and frosty.
He drew the sun.

"Gregory," said the teacher. "Please come to the front
of the room and draw a circle for the class."

Gregory drew a circle.
"It looks like a flat tire," said Donald, laughing.

Gregory sat down.
An ant walked across his arithmetic paper.

Gregory drew a city for the ant to live in.
When it was finished, there wasn't any room for the answers to the arithmetic problems.

At recess Gregory watched some big machines
working across the street.

They looked like iron dinosaurs
fighting in the dust.

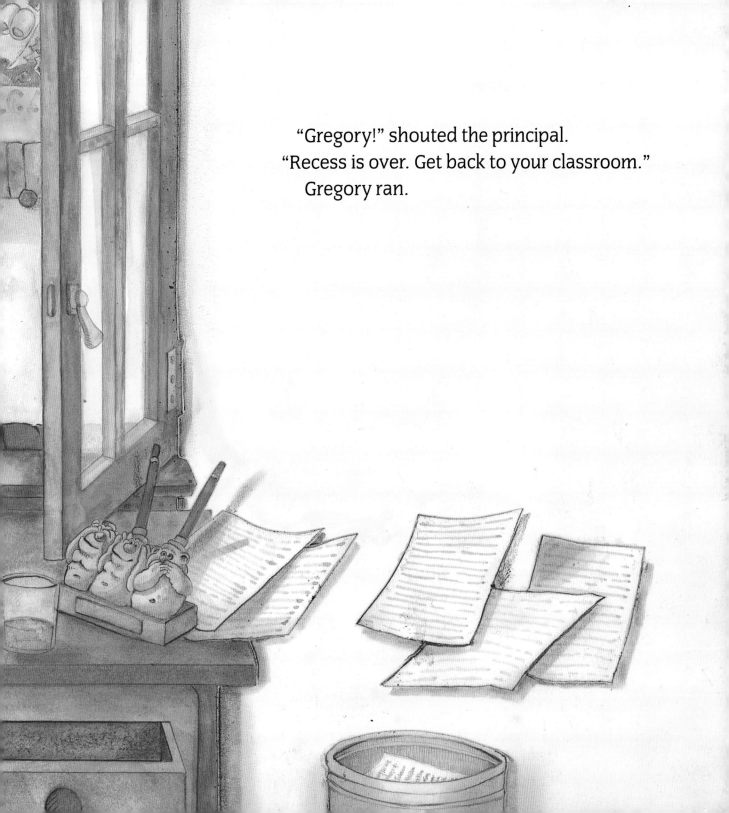

"Gregory!" shouted the principal.
"Recess is over. Get back to your classroom."
Gregory ran.

"We're waiting," said the teacher.

Gregory took out his crayons. He set them neatly
at the top of his desk. He put his best eraser next
to his favorite pencil.

Adrienne gave Gregory a piece of drawing paper.
Gregory brushed it off—

and his crayons fell on the floor.

"Come on, come on," moaned Curtis. "We don't have all…"

"Today," said the teacher, "we're going to draw a vase and flowers. We call this a 'still life.' Please begin."

Gregory drew his picture carefully.
    He turned the picture upside down
and added shadows.
    Upside down the flowers looked like
flames, and the vase looked like
a rocket ship.
    Gregory added fins.

He drew spinning planets and flashing comets in
the night sky. He filled the darkness with tiny stars.
When it was finished, he signed his name.

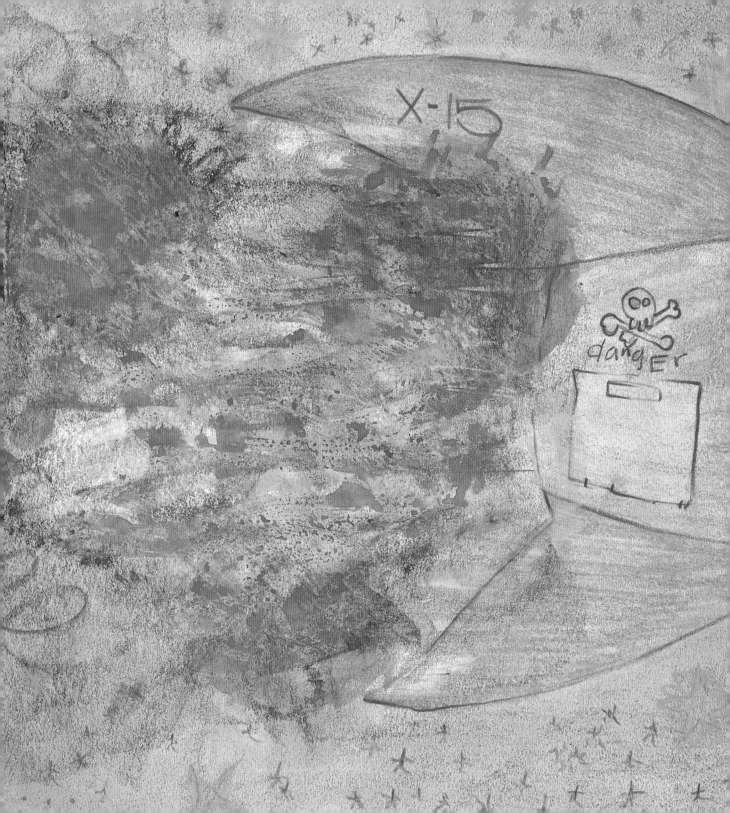

The bell rang.
"Now you're going to get it," whispered Donald. "You were supposed to be drawing flowers, not a stupid rocket ship!"

"Time to go," said the teacher. "Adrienne, please collect the pictures."

Adrienne stopped at Donald's desk.

"Gosh," she said. "I didn't know your baby brother could draw THIS good!"

"Very funny," Donald grunted.

Gregory put his crayons away.

"Don't forget your homework," said the teacher.
Gregory opened his desk and found his homework.
He folded it and put it in his lunch box.

Gregory walked down the hall. He heard the teacher
call his name.
"Gregory," she said, "your lunch box!"
Gregory walked back to his desk and got his lunch box.

He climbed on the bus and sat next to the window.
Just as the bus started, it stopped.

"WHOA!" shouted Adrienne. She jumped on the bus
and flopped down next to Gregory.

"That was *sooo* close! I had to help the teacher put
up our pictures," she sighed. "You should see them.
Most of them look pretty good. Mine's so-so. But yours—

you should see it. The teacher put it right in the
middle of all the flowers. It's beautiful. The teacher
said so. I love it. How do you make those stars?
Do you want a bite of my Crunch Bar?"

Gregory smiled and bit off a piece of the candy bar.

He touched the window.
The glass was cold and frosty.
Gregory drew a circle.

It was perfect.